MW00929908

THE MIRRORS
OF NARCISSUS

Nicole Kavner Miller

Manse Street Stories
Huntington, NY

Copyright 2013 by Nicole Kavner Miller
All Rights Reserved

Manse Street Stories, a division of Beyond the Story
P.O. Box 172
Huntington, NY 11743

ISBN-13: 978-1484984604
ISBN-10: 1484984609

2

To all the mirrors in my life, with love.

1

With bow and quiver slung casually over one shoulder, Narcissus gazed at the olive trees surrounding him, breathing in their fragrant scent.

"Mmmmmmmm…" he breathed in deeply.

"Mmm…" came a female voice from behind him.

"Stop doing that!" he replied with annoyance.

"Doing that!" the voice responded.

"You heard me!" Narcissus warned.

"Heard me!" the voice, once again, offered.

"I'm not interested."

"Interested."

"*Go away!*" he shouted.

"*Away!*" she replied.

Narcissus turned away from the young girl who had been following him, and walked the mile toward home. It had been a long day of hunting and he was exhausted.

As he reached his street, he saw a familiar sight. *Oh brother!* He thought to himself. *Not him too?* At his front door stood Ameinias, a young man who professed his love for Narcissus almost daily.

"Ameinias, go home!" Narcissus ordered him.

"I can't," Ameinias cried. "I love you and I'll always love you."

"Well, I don't love you! But if you want something of mine, here," Narcissus thrust the hilt of his sword toward Ameinias. "Take my sword. That's all I can offer you." And with that, Narcissus entered his home, shut the door on Ameinias' downcast face, and greeted his mother, Liriope, who was sitting by the fire.

"Hello, love," she greeted him. Then, noticing the distressed look on Narcissus' face, beckoned for him to join her by the hearth. "What's troubling you, my beautiful, handsome boy?"

"Mother, I can't seem to go anywhere without these young men and nymphs declaring their love for me. None of them interest me. I simply want to hunt and walk along in the woods, spending time on my own, doing my own thing."

"Narcissus, it's only fitting that all should fall in love with you, my gorgeous, clever boy. But you're right, none of them is indeed good enough for you."

"That's what I keep telling them!" Narcissus cried. "And there's this annoying girl near the caves who keeps repeating the last words I say. It's maddening!"

"Yes, Echo, well it's a lot better than her previous incessant gossiping! That girl could talk and talk and talk… Don't worry yourself, my darling. Just stay here with me, my love. Mother understands."

"How can you understand? You don't know what it's like to have people swooning all over you every day! Being the object of desire! Really, mother, how could you possibly understand? Please just stick to what you do best. Is my dinner ready yet?" Narcissus rose from the hearth and lay down on the soft pelts in the corner. "Please just wake me when my dinner is ready."

* * * * *

The next morning, Narcissus awoke early, grabbed his bow, and headed out into the crisp morning air. But before he could take a single step, there across his doorstep, lay Ameinias. His body bloodied and broken, Ameinias lay dead, having driven Narcissus' sword deep into his heart. Attached to the sword was a note:

"MY DEAREST NARCISSUS,
I CANNOT LIVE WITHOUT YOUR
LOVE ONE MOMENT LONGER. BY
YOUR TENDER SWORD, I WOULD
HAVE GIVEN YOU MY HEART
FOREVER, BUT ALAS, BY YOUR
SHARPENED SWORD, I DIE.

MY LOVE FOR YOU IS ETERNAL,
AMEINIAS

P.S. I DID ASK THE GODS TO CURSE
YOU THOUGH, SORRY ABOUT
THAT, MY LOVE..."

Narcissus was unsure what to make of this. He had given the young man a perfectly good blade. What a waste! Narcissus reached down and grabbed a hold of the sword's hilt. With one long tug, he pulled the sword out of the young man's body, and blood poured from the gaping wound in Ameinias' heart.

Narcissus looked down once more at the body and shook his head, "Well, at least he won't be troubling me any more."

He rinsed the sword off in a nearby brook, and started off in search of wild boar.

* * * * *

As Helios made his way to the halfway point across the sky, Narcissus sat down to eat a lunch of beer and berries, but he noticed that he was not alone. The young girl from the day before was watching him.

"Who are you?" Narcissus asked her.

"Are you," she replied.

"Are you Echo?"

"Echo?"

"Why do you keep doing that?" Narcissus was getting increasingly agitated.

"Doing that?"

"Yes, that."

"That."

Narcissus rolled his eyes and went back to his lunch. Echo came closer and sat down next to him on some rocks. He turned his body away from her so that she was no longer in his sightline, and there she remained for the rest of his meal.

When Narcissus rose to leave, the young girl stood up as well, her face beaming with light and love.

Realizing that she might follow him home, Narcissus said sternly, "Oh no, you can't come with me."

"Come with me," she replied.

"I'm not coming with you!" Narcissus replied, confused that now she wanted him to go home with her.

"Coming with you!" she responded.

"What? No, you wretched creature," Narcissus exclaimed.

"Wretched creature," Echo said sadly.

"Stay away from me and don't bother me again," Narcissus demanded, as he turned away from her and stomped off.

"Bother me again," Echo replied, as tears slowly ran down her cheeks.

* * * * *

On the other side of the pond from where Narcissus and Echo stood, Aphrodite and Nemesis silently appeared, observing the upsetting little scene.

"What is wrong with that boy?" Aphrodite asked her companion. "I sent him two perfectly good potential love interests, and what does he do? He drives one to suicide and the other he spurns over and over again. We must fix this."

"Yes, I've had numerous pleas for justice from the victims of that self-centered boy," Nemesis replied. "Just last night before

Ameinias took his own life, he sent me the most eloquent plea, 'Dearest goddess, the one who balances the right and wrong, who lifts up the downtrodden and puts hubris in its place. Please, I beg of you, show Narcissus what he's done to me. Make him feel the pain I've been suffering! Make him fall in love and know the frustration of being unable to be with his Beloved. And, because I do love him so, dear goddess of justice, please give him a chance at redemption, as well.'"

"Redemption, hmph! As if a man like that could ever change!" Aphrodite declared.

"I have an idea," Nemesis replied. "He needs to know the pain he's caused others, right? Then, let him fall in love with the one person he could never truly have."

"Who is that, dear sister?" Aphrodite inquired.

"Himself. When next he sees his own image, he will fall deeply and madly in love with himself."

"That should do," Aphrodite agreed with a smirk.

"And so shall it be…" Nemesis waved her hand toward Narcissus' retreating figure, casting the curse, and changing the course of Narcissus' life forever.

* * * * *

Narcissus slowed his pace and turned around. Echo was gone. *Thank the gods!* He thought to himself. Thirsty and seeing a lovely little pond up ahead, Narcissus dropped his bow, quiver, and other belongings to the ground and bent down to take a drink.

As his eyes looked into the crystal clear water, he caught sight of the most beautiful being he'd ever seen. He felt as if he'd been shot in the heart with Eros' arrow. There in the pond was a handsome and totally irresistible young man.

"Well, hello!" Narcissus cried out.

The young man responded as well, but silently. Narcissus saw his mouth move and watched as the young man's arms reached out for him, just as Narcissus reached his arms out to the young man.

"I've never been struck by such love before!" Narcissus declared. "My heart is beating like a thousand horses galloping freely into the wild. Oh, my Beloved, please tell me your name!"

But as excited and animated as the Beloved's image was, there was no audible response.

"Can't you speak, my Beloved? Are you mute?"

Narcissus paused to listen for a reply. With none forthcoming, he nevertheless could not take his gaze from the visage of the beautiful man.

* * * * *

Days passed and Narcissus remained, faithfully lying by the pond's edge; whispering words of love and devotion to his perfect love. He had run out of food by the morning of the second day, and he dared not take a drink from the pond again, as when he did, his Beloved disappeared.

Liriope, concerned about her son's absence, came looking for him on the third day. Finding her son staring ceaselessly into the pond, she urged him to return home so he could eat and rest.

"No, mother, I can't leave my Beloved here. I've finally found someone worthy of my love and affection, someone who reaches out to me with love, and offers me the moon and the stars, as I do him."

"But it's just your reflection in the water, my son. All you see is yourself in it," Liriope replied.

"No, mother, can't you see him? He's perfect! Why can't you just understand that I need to be with him?" Narcissus pleaded.

Liriope grabbed a hold of Narcissus' arm, and pulled him towards her, "Come now, Narcissus, this is silliness. Come home with me now!"

"No, mother!" Narcissus said angrily, as he pushed her away with such force that she tumbled backwards to the ground. "Just leave us alone! Leave me alone with my Beloved and don't come back!"

Liriope shakily got herself to her feet, and wondered what she should do next. Should she run and get some men from the village? Should she go and find Tireisias? He had warned her against Narcissus "knowing himself." Is this what he meant? Weeping for her confused and delusional boy, she walked home and debated what she should do.

* * * * *

As the sun rose on the fourth day, hungry and dehydrated, Narcissus pleaded once more with his Beloved.

"Embrace me, my love. Why do you vanish when all I want to do is hold you in my arms?"

The Beloved's face in the pond mirrored back to Narcissus all of his love and entreaties; but still, there was no audible response.

"It's true, then, isn't it? What my mother suggested may actually be the truth? Are you only a reflection of me? Reason would allow for me to stand up and retreat; to return home and forget about this misadventure, and yet, I can't. My love for you burns brighter than ever."

And so, he remained there until his body could take no more. Thirst and hunger stopped troubling poor Narcissus, and with his last breath, he lovingly exhaled, "*Beloved*," and his newly inanimate body tumbled into the welcoming water.

2

As he plunged deeper and deeper into the watery abyss, Narcissus felt his body separate from his spirit, and watched as his corpse, now bloated with freshwater, floated up to the surface of the pristine pond. To his wonderment, his old body began to shrink and transfigure, and in its place, a beautiful yellow flower emerged at the surface of the water. As Narcissus pondered this surprising phenomenon, his spirit continued to sink effortlessly to the bottom. Lying on the grassy floor of the pond was a magnificent, glittering thing. He made his way to the curious object and examined its peculiar shape. It was tall, as tall as he was, and oblong-shaped, and stood on what appeared to be a pedestal. Most splendid of all, Narcissus realized, was that he could once again see his Beloved's face in the glass.

The standing mirror revealed to Narcissus a full-sized image of his love. As he reached out to embrace this image, he found his arms drawn deeper into the mirror. He could feel his hands grasped by another's.

"Beloved!"

As Narcissus gleefully stepped through the mirror and into the waiting arms of his lover, he instead came face to face with Hermes.

"Hi, Narcissus," Hermes greeted him.

"Wait, what are you doing here?" Narcissus asked the god.

"It's my job. I make sure that all the souls, whether eager or wayward, find their way to Hades."

"You're kidding, right?" Narcissus pulled his hands away from Hermes, and turned around to face the mirror he had just come through. But alas, he could only see the tarnished opaque back.

"It's not fair!" Narcissus pouted aloud to Hermes. "My Beloved has disappeared and I'll never find another quite so beautiful or so perfect again!"

And with that, he turned around and found himself next to a black and foreboding river. Having lost sight of his Beloved once again struck annoyance and longing into Narcissus' heart, and he threw himself down petulantly on the banks of the ancient river.

As he began to wail and tantrum at the heartless acts of the Fates, he caught a quick sideways glance of his Beloved again.

"Oh!" Narcissus' sharp intake of breath caught him off guard, "You look different, but I still recognize you! Be with me forever, my love."

"Shut up, you moron, and get in the boat!" a gruff voice rudely interrupted his thoughts.

Narcissus tore his glance away from his Beloved long enough to see a shriveled old man in a black patchwork cloak crooking a finger at him.

"You heard me, boy. Your passage has already been paid by Tiriesias, that blind old bugger. I'm into him for 4,000 kroner. By Zeus, he cheats worse than Hermes," the old man said, gesturing at the trickster god.

"He's blind, Charon," Hermes reminded him.

"He may be blind, but he still cheats! You've heard him, 'Oh, no, Charon. I don't use my powers of the Oracle to win at Gin Rummy,' he says. Yeah, right! Well, what are you waiting for," turning now to Narcissus, "a golden ticket? Get in the frickin' boat!"

Narcissus had never been spoken to this way before. This peculiar, desiccated creature's behavior was so foreign to Narcissus' normal aesthetic experience that he sat in momentary paralytic shock on the riverbank.

"Oh for Hades' sake!" Charon reached one bony arm toward Narcissus and lifted him by his hair into the boat.

Coming back to his senses, Narcissus began to protest leaving the riverbank.

"I found my Beloved again! Look! There, in the dark water. I see him! I can't leave him behind! I must be with him!"

Charon sighed the sigh of a parent whose child insists on riding their tricycle repeatedly into the wall—over and over and over and over....

"I tell you what, boy," Charon began, knowing that there was only one way to get this boat ride over with. "I'll throw this rope into the water and your 'Beloved' can grab a hold of it and follow the boat along as we go."

This sounded reasonable to Narcissus. If the boatman was going to be fair-minded about letting his Beloved come with him, then he was happy.

As Narcissus boarded the boat, Hermes, his job completed, vanished in a gust of wind.

* * * * *

The boat neared the far shore of the dark and murky river, as Narcissus continued to smile adoringly at his reflection in the water.

"GRRRRRRR..." a mighty growl suddenly erupted in the air.

Then two mighty growls thundered forth, and then a third one, which turned into a howl that chilled the spine.

"That'll be Cerberus welcoming you to the other side. Don't mind him, he's all bark. Unless, of course, you try to *leave* the Underworld," Charon continued with a crooked smirk, "'Cause then he'll rip you into little tiny pieces that he'll gnash up into bloody applesauce in his massive sets of teeth. But, I wouldn't worry about that too much. OK, this is your stop. Good luck and all that!"

Narcissus stared at the colossal tri-headed dog in front of him. He had heard tales of this guardian of the threshold of Hades, but never in all his imaginings would he have envisioned the massiveness of this fierce and sinewy beast. One by one, the vicious heads swung close to Narcissus' face, so close that he could smell the festering stink of death on them. Snorting and growling, they surveyed Narcissus standing before them. Narcissus trembled to his very core and found his feet glued to the bottom of the boat with abject terror.

"Go on, go on...you big wuss! The entrance is over there," Charon prodded.

Narcissus found the strength to lift one leg off the ground, but instead of walking forward, he began walking backwards in the boat.

"Oh no you don't!" Charon warned. "Forward is the only path. I tell ya what..."

Charon reached into his cloak and pulled out a tiny shard of mirror he had tucked away in a deep pocket.

"Take this. I keep it for those times when a tragic young virgin is about to make the crossing. Gotta look my best for those sweet young things," Charon mused, running his fingers over the three hairs combed sideways on the top of his bald and spotted head.

"Look, look in the reflection. What do you see?"

Narcissus gazed into the shard of mirror placed in his palm.

"My Beloved," he sighed.

"That's right. Keep your eyes on your Beloved and you'll have nothing to fear."

Charon looked at Cerberus and winked. Cerberus' heads grinned and rolled their eyes, they'd seen it all before, but this was a hoot. The three-headed monster clomped back onto the far end of the shore, away from the entrance to the underworld and sat down. The middle head yawned a big gawping yawn, while the head on the left cleaned a paw, and the head on the right licked his giant nether regions.

Narcissus, cradling the shard of mirror in his hand, began his journey into the Underworld, unconcerned and unaware of his surroundings. Filled with love and lust, he walked, glass in hand, with his projection.

3

Narcissus briefly glanced away from his Beloved in the mirror shard, and gazed up at the enormous decorative gateway in front of him. It was a monstrous thing to behold. At the top was a relief of Hades and Persephone beaming brightly at all who stood beneath it. Underneath them were carved images of people cavorting merrily in the Elysian Fields. Beneath that was a landscape of Asphodel Meadow, it was simple, yet non-threatening. And on the bottom of the gate, horrific and ghastly creatures were seen frozen, screaming in torment. Narcissus felt a chill run down his spine, as he thought that he recognized one of the images toward the bottom of the door.

"Is that Antagonis?" he wondered aloud. "Why would they carve an image of him on this great gate?"

"It's my penance," a gravelly voice responded, as the face on the door began to move.

"Antagonis? Is that actually you?" Narcissus replied with repulsion.

"Yep, my old hunting buddy. This is my eternal punishment. It happens," he said with a shrug. "Excuse me one second, OK?" Antagonis then let out the most blood-curdling scream Narcissus had ever heard.

Narcissus took two steps backwards, almost dropping his shard of mirror.

"What happened?" he asked. "Why are you screaming?"

"I'm in agony," Antagonis replied. "I can never leave this door, and I can never actually enter Hades. I watch endless numbers of people arrive, some joyful, some terrified, but me, I have to sit here and get horrified looks all day long. Not to mention...I have to deal with Herbie." Antagonis glanced upwards to the face above him.

"It's Herbavoris, and it's not my fault!" Herbie cried out. "I can't help it if my knee is stuck in your back. It's not like I planned it that way. Or wanted it to be that way. Or asked for it to be that way. Or..."

"Enough!" Antagonis yelled at Herbie. "You see what I have to deal with?" he implored of Narcissus.

"Fine!" Herbie responded. Turning toward Narcissus, he asked, "So...why are you here. What's your story, Morning Glory?"

"I'm here…I mean…I'm not sure. I am completely and desperately in love with my Beloved though, look!" Narcissus held up the mirror shard. "You can see him if you look in here."

Narcissus positioned the mirror so that Antagonis and Herbie could see the image of his Beloved.

"AAAAAAAAAAAAAAAAAAA! Put it away! Put it away!" screamed Antagonis and Herbie.

"What's the matter?" Narcissus said, as he turned the mirror back toward himself and once again saw the loving image of his Beloved.

"Oh my Zeus! Oh my Apollo! Oh my, oh my!" Herbie moaned and carried on.

"Why would you show us that?" Antagonis added. "That's horrible!"

"What do you mean? Why would you say that about him?" Narcissus said with surprise.

"You showed us ourselves, you jerky. It's bad enough that we're stuck here on the gate, but we didn't need that visual," Antagonis grumpily replied.

"But I don't understand…" Narcissus mumbled.

"You're in love with what you see in the mirror? You're in love with yourself!" Antagonis said incredulously. "Ha! That's rich. You were always pretty self-involved weren't you? I mean, we went hunting together and everything, but you always had to pose with your kill. You made me paint a picture of you smiling above a boar, or a goat, or whatever. You were always in love with yourself, ya dummy."

Narcissus stared in bewilderment at Antagonis. "Why must you be so cruel? I'm here in Hades, and I'll never walk in the forests again, or hunt, or have my portrait painted. Why must you make me feel worse?"

"I don't know, just comes naturally to me, I guess," he replied.

"Yeah, he can't help it," Herbie added. "Hey Antagonis, I think we need to scream again."

"Yeah, you're right. Narcissus, you better get inside the gates and see what the judges have in store for you. Maybe you could join us here on the gate?"

And with that, the massive doors swung open and the faces on the door began to wail and scream. Narcissus held the mirror in front of him as he walked through. Focus on your Beloved, Charon had said. It'll be all right.

As the doors to Hades closed behind him, Narcissus could still hear the intermittent screams from the faces on the door. As he started down a long dark hallway, he thought he heard Herbie say, "He's gorgeous!"

"Shut up, ya dummy," the raspy voice replied.

* * * * *

Narcissus wandered through the dark and dusty fields of Asphodel. Through the haze, he began to make out the forms of others, as they wandered around in small groups, talking.

"Hey, new guy!" a man's voice carried over the dusk-colored air to Narcissus.

Narcissus turned around to face a man in his 60s, who was well dressed and carrying a watering can.

"Are you talking to me?" Narcissus inquired.

"Yes, I'm talking to you! Stop trampling on my garden!" Narcissus glanced down and saw a drawing of three flowers drawn into the dirt under his feet.

"Those aren't real flowers," Narcissus replied, annoyed.

"Yes they are, and they're mine!" the man countered.

"Well, can't you just draw new ones?" Narcissus responded logically. "They're only pictures of flowers, it's not like they're alive."

"Images are living things, stupid," the man cried angrily. "I created them, so they're real to me. They're my images. They belong to me!"

Narcissus had no response to this clearly unhinged man. He was perplexed, and couldn't understand how the man could believe that what he saw was real, when it was obviously only delusion.

Walking briskly away, Narcissus noticed a few people waiting to speak to a very official-looking fellow behind a podium. Ah, that's probably the way to the Elysian Fields, Narcissus thought, confident that a man of his attractiveness and charisma would certainly end up there.

Narcissus walked to the front of the gathered people and asked the attendant, "What happens now?"

"You need to get in line. Wait your turn," the attendant replied.

Narcissus looked behind him and, for the first time, noticed an enormous line that snaked back all the way to the front gate.

"What, you mean this line?" Narcissus asked incredulously. "I don't want to waste my time on line. The Elysian Fields, right? Just tell me how to get there and I'll be on my way."

"Listen, buddy, you're no more special than all the rest of them. Just get in line," the attendant turned his attention away from Narcissus and toward the female shade standing in front of him.

Narcissus glanced into his mirror and found solace in the reflected indignation. He walked to the back of the line containing thousands of people, and waited.

And waited.

And waited.

Narcissus, again, left the line and walked to the front.

"Seriously," he addressed the attendant. "Why do I have to wait here with all of these people?"

"Where else exactly do you have to be right now?" the attendant responded.

Narcissus had no response to this. He turned around again and walked back to where he had been standing.

As he assumed his previous position, the shade that had been standing behind him glared at him and said, "Uh, excuse me! Just what exactly do you think you're doing?"

"I guess I have to wait on this line like the rest of you," Narcissus responded.

"Oh, poor baby, you have to wait like the rest of us," another man replied from the line. "You left the line, now you have to go to the back."

"But there's at least another thousand people who've joined the line since I left it."

"Boohoo to you! You snooze, you lose," the man who had been behind Narcissus said. "You're not getting back in line here, that's for sure."

"Fine," Narcissus sighed heavily. Why was everyone being so disagreeable? He thought to himself.

* * * * *

As Narcissus neared the front of the line, he listened to the conversations of the people in front of him.

"I just don't remember it exactly," the woman said. "There were some baby owls that were stranded in a fire in the olive grove. They couldn't fly yet and I remember climbing up to get to their nest. I reached out my hand to loosen it from the tree limb before the fire engulfed us, and then, that's it, everything went black."

"Why'd you bother," the man said. "Why would you risk your life for birds?"

"They were helpless and I just couldn't stand it if they had burnt to death so young," the woman replied. "I don't know what happened to their mother. Perhaps she had perished in the fire already."

"Wait, what grove were you in?" the man asked. "It wasn't the one near Parnassus, was it?"

"Yes, how did you know…" the woman asked, already suspecting the reply.

"I'd been hunting there, killed myself a gorgeous owl. I wanted to use the feathers for a new cloak I was making."

"You mean you killed those poor little babies' mother for a cloak?" the woman asked with disgust.

The man shrugged, and said, "Yeah, probably. I had already skinned it, and was cooking it for dinner that night, when an ember flicked out of the fire and caught on some nearby brush. Within seconds, my clothes were on fire and I was screaming in agony! And then I ended up here. Kind of bummed about the cloak, though."

As the man finished his tale, the line had moved forward, and he was now standing in front of the attendant.

"Name," asked the attendant.

"Vainglorious," the man replied. The attendant took a few moments to search for his name on the chart, and then instructed him to step inside the courtroom on the right.

As Vainglorious disappeared into the room, Narcissus turned to the woman in front of him and asked, "What happens in there?"

"I'm not entirely sure," she responded, "but I think the three judges are in there. They decide whether we stay here, or go on to the Elysian Fields or down to Tartarus."

"I already know where I'm going," Narcissus replied, and he looked into his mirror shard at his Beloved's reflection for reassurance.

A few moments later, Vainglorious emerged from the courtroom, his hands tied with rope, and being led by a guard.

"She had it in for me!" he exclaimed.

"Who?" asked the woman.

"Athena! She actually appeared in the room; she never comes down here. She asked them to send me to Tartarus for hunting and killing one of her owls. She was raising those owls. Who knew?" Vainglorious was led away by his tether.

"Name," the attendant asked the woman in front of Narcissus.

"Compassia," she replied, and the attendant gestured for her to step inside the courtroom.

Narcissus began to worry. He went hunting all the time, though he had never hunted one of Athena's sacred owls. Everyone knew that Athena was very protective of those birds. What an idiot, he thought to himself, and he watched as Vainglorious was dropped into the dark pit of Tartarus.

A few minutes went by, and Compassia emerged from the room, escorted by Athena.

"They were her owl babies. Goddess Athena said such beautiful, eloquent things in there," Compassia smiled at Narcissus, as she walked toward the golden gates of the Elysian Fields. "Good luck to you in your judgment proceedings," she called out to him, as she walked away.

"Name," the attendant asked.

"Narcissus."

The attendant gestured toward the courtroom, and Narcissus turned and stepped toward the doors. As he put his hand on the handle, he affixed his most winning smile upon his face, and walked through the door.

4

Narcissus glanced around at the assembled figures. At the apex of the room stood a small rise, where the three judges, Rhadamanthus, Minos, and Aeacus sat on impressive thrones. *After all, they had been kings when they were alive,* Narcissus thought to himself, *and they still looked quite king-like, indeed.*

"Narcissus," announced another attendant inside the room.

"Step forward, Narcissus," King Aeacus directed.

Stepping forward toward the king, Narcissus gave a perfunctory bow.

"King Aeacus, good to see you!" Narcissus began. "Is it you who'll be sending me to Elysium?"

"Not quite yet," the King responded. "So tell us, have you led a good life?"

"Well enough, I suppose. I've often enjoyed a good hunt, and I've lived as I wanted to. I have no regrets," Narcissus replied with a broad smile.

"No regrets?" King Aeacus asked.

"Nope," responded Narcissus quickly.

"Are you familiar with a young nymph named Echo?"

"Echo?" Narcissus thought aloud. "No, who's Echo?"

"Who's Echo?" bellowed King Minos, causing Narcissus to tremble slightly. "Do you remember a young maiden who could only repeat the last words you said?"

"Oh yes!" Narcissus remembered. "That must be that annoying girl by the pond. Yes, I remember her. What does she have to do with anything?"

"She offered you her love and you dismissed her, turning her away and showing her no respect at all," King Aeacus responded.

"But she was just a nuisance!" Narcissus cried. "I just wanted to be left alone."

"And Ameinias, what about him? He took his life after he was rejected by you time and time again," King Minos added.

"He's the one who chose to kill himself. I tried to let him down gently, I gave him a sword!"

"A sword?"

"Yes, it was a nice sword, in fact. As a sort of consolation prize," Narcissus replied.

"This one's all yours, Aeacus," King Rhadamanthus mumbled with a chuckle to King Aeacus.

"But do you not feel any remorse for having hurt Echo and Ameinias, and countless others?" King Aeacus probed further.

"What do you mean *hurt them*? I was honest with them. Their feelings are their problem."

"No empathy," stated King Rhadamanthus.

Both King Minos and King Aeacus nodded their heads in agreement.

"Do you think that you were worthy of their love?" King Aeacus asked Narcissus.

"Of course, I'm worthy. I'm beautiful, everyone says so," Narcissus replied.

"What I meant was, is your heart worthy of the love of another?"

Narcissus looked confused, "My heart is as beautiful as the rest of me. From far and wide, people come just to gaze at me, but I try to pay them no mind. I'm a fabulous hunter, and I need to have a brave heart for that. It's the bravest heart around, my mother tells me. So, yes, I'm worthy. No one has ever told me otherwise."

The three kings huddled together for a moment, deep in discussion. As Narcissus waited impatiently, he glanced around the room and was taken aback when he saw the image of his Beloved in the glass of an adjacent door. His heart beat faster as he walked over to the door and gazed lovingly at his own image.

"See what I mean?" King Rhadamanthus whispered to King Minos.

King Minos nodded his head, and replied, "He never learned the lesson that Nemesis tried to teach him."

"He's un-teachable," King Aeacus added.

"Perhaps," King Minos responded.

As the kings discussed his fate amongst themselves, they failed to notice that Narcissus had reached out to embrace his Beloved in the mirror and, as in the pond, his arms disappeared into the depths of the mirror. Intrigued, Narcissus stepped into the fluid image, and beheld the strangest scene he'd ever seen.

5

Narcissus gazed around the chamber he had stepped into, as strange men with animal heads and odd clothing turned toward him and stared. *Um, this is different*, Narcissus thought to himself. *Am I in Tartarus, in the presence of some strange monsters yet unseen by the people on the surface?*

"What is this? Who are you?" a creature with a man's body and the head of a bird, said to him.

"I'm Narcissus, and I was reaching for my Beloved when I ended up here. I didn't come here to get involved in whatever it is you're doing there," gesturing to the enormous set of scales in the center of the room. It appeared that there was a soft white feather on one side of the balance, and some sort of human organ on the other. He wanted no part of whatever sacrificial ritual was going on. "I must have made a mistake somewhere."

A strange and vicious-looking beast growled at Narcissus. It looked like a combination of a lion, a hippopotamus, and a crocodile.

"What is that?" Narcissus asked fearfully, as he surveyed the fearsome creature.

"That's Ammut, the Soul Eater," replied the man with the bird head.

Narcissus reached behind him and felt along the wall of the chamber for the passageway through which he had come. *Soul eater, huh?* Narcissus wondered. *What sort of deepest, darkest Hades is this?* Unable to find the way out, he reached into his pocket to retrieve the shard of mirror the boatman had given him.

"Keep my eyes on my Beloved and I'll be OK," he mumbled to himself, but unfortunately, the shard of mirror was gone. *I must have lost it when I walked through the wall,* he realized with horror.

"Come forward, spirit, and let us judge your righteousness," said a man on a throne, overseeing the proceedings. "I'm Osiris, King of the Underworld and it's time for the weighing of your heart."

"I thought Hades was king of the Underworld," Narcissus muttered.

"Come forward!" Osiris insisted.

As Narcissus tentatively walked toward the scales, he noticed odd pictures and writing on the walls.

"What's all of that?" he asked.

"They're spells to assist you in the afterlife," replied the man with the bird head.

"Spells? I was under some sort of spell at the end of my life; could your spells allow me to finally embrace my Beloved?"

A man with a jackal head on a human body reached toward Narcissus, and in one swift move, snatched Narcissus' heart from inside his chest. Narcissus stared in amazement at his heart, as he watched it being placed onto one side of the scales. A new white feather floated through the room and landed on the other side. The scales began to wobble up and down, until they came to rest just slightly less than balanced. His heart was heavier than the feather.

"What does that mean?" Narcissus asked those assembled there. The sound the lion-hippo-crocodile creature made in reply was terrifying.

"You have been judged as less than righteous," announced the bird-headed man. The verdict is the devouring of your heart and soul. There will be no afterlife for you. You will, as of this moment, cease to exist."

The creature, Ammut, licked his gruesome lips and moved his snout closer to Narcissus' heart, delighted that he would have a tasty meal.

"Wait!" yelled Hermes, as he emerged through the hidden passageway in the wall. "He's one of ours! Please return his heart. There's been some sort of mistake."

"But he has already been judged!" announced the bird-headed man.

"Thoth, with all due respect, Queen Persephone herself has asked me to find and retrieve him."

"Persephone? How is the queen these days?"

"She's good. Finally settling in, it was a difficult adjustment period, and everything. You're looking well, it's been a while."

"Yes, I've been using those ochre mud packs from the Nile..."

"Excuse me," Narcissus interrupted. "This is all very nice and everything, but you're forgetting about me. What about me? What's going to happen to me?"

Both Hermes and Thoth turned toward Narcissus, and then back to face each other.

"You can have him," Thoth replied, with a knowing look. "Anubis, give him back his heart. Have you seen what's in his psyche, Hermes? It's a mess in there."

"I know," Hermes agreed.

"Stop discussing me like I'm not even here? I'm right here!" Narcissus cried out. "And by right here…I mean…where am I?" Narcissus turned to Hermes for an explanation.

"You're in Egypt, Narcissus. You went through the sacred passageway. Apparently, the attendant tried to stop you but he couldn't, so they summoned me. This is Thoth, the god of wisdom and magic," Hermes said, gesturing to the bird-headed man. "He's my mirror."

"He's your what?" Narcissus asked.

"My mirror. When I look at him, I see me very clearly."

"And vice versa, my friend," Thoth replied.

Narcissus stood there with a blank expression on his face.

"Don't worry your pretty little head about it," Hermes continued. "It will all be revealed soon enough."

"And my Beloved? He's disappeared again. Will you help me find him?"

"Yes, Narcissus, he's through the sacred passageway from whence you came. Come along, we shall see him again," Hermes comforted Narcissus, and guided him back toward the wall of the chamber.

"There's no door here," Narcissus cried, bewildered.

"Reach your arms out toward the wall where you see the picture of the wavy lines enclosed in a square," Hermes instructed.

"What is that?" he asked.

"It's a She, the symbol for water or pond," Hermes replied, and as Narcissus touched the picture, his arms began to move through the wall.

"That's amaz…" Narcissus began, but he did not have time to finish, as Hermes shoved him unceremoniously through the sacred passageway.

Hermes turned and smiled at Thoth, "See you again, my dear friend," and vanished through the passageway back into Hades.

6

Narcissus stumbled through the wall, and found himself in an enormous room filled with a thousand mirrors. In every mirror, he saw his Beloved, who looked at him with much awe and amazement.

"But...but...how could there be so many of you?" Narcissus said in wonderment. Narcissus turned all the way around, gazing at each vision of his Beloved, in turn. Reaching toward one of the images, he was disappointed to find that he could not touch his lover. He ran toward another mirror and tried again, this time hitting his head against the glass material.

"Ouch!" he cried, rubbing his forehead. Narcissus began to pout at his constant frustration.

He gazed up again at his Beloved's image and was distraught to notice that his Beloved was now looking at him with a frustrated look as well; his Beloved was also rubbing his head in pain.

"Why are you in pain?" Narcissus asked. "Because I'm in pain?"

The Beloved made no reply, it merely continued to look more and more upset and animated. Narcissus began to run around the room, flitting from one mirror to another, searching for one in which the Beloved would gaze at him with love and longing. All he could see were panicked visions of his Beloved, also running around the room, looking for him. It was all very confusing and distressing. Narcissus collapsed onto his knees on the floor of the room. His head in his hands, he began to sob. *Nothing is making any sense anymore*, he wailed.

Just then, Hermes emerged from one of the mirrors.

"You went the wrong way again!" Hermes reprimanded him. "What am I going to do with you?"

Narcissus lifted his head from his hands and looked at Hermes.

"You were supposed to go straight all the way through the passage. You stepped to the right instead," Hermes added.

"I have no idea what you're talking about," Narcissus replied wearily.

"Come, it's time that you found out your fate in the afterlife. The three judges are waiting for you."

"But what's the meaning of this room, Hermes?" Narcissus wanted to know.

"It shows you what you offer of yourself to the world, sent back to you one-thousand-fold."

"But it shows my Beloved surrounding me," Narcissus said.

"Yes, but did you notice that when you expressed love, the images expressed love, and when you expressed distress the images expressed distress too?" Hermes asked.

"Yes, but it was all too much to take in," Narcissus began to wail. Hermes reached for Narcissus' arm and escorted him back to the judges.

7

Narcissus re-entered the courtroom, and immediately felt the penetrating gaze of the three judges.

"Step forward," King Minos said to Narcissus. "Did you enjoy your little sojourn?"

"There was a soul-eating beast there, and he almost ate my heart!" Narcissus cried.

"Ah, Ammut," King Minos chuckled. "I've always found him to be a curious creature. Did you learn anything about yourself while you were in the Duat?"

"Well…" Narcissus began tentatively, "They said that my heart was heavy and because of that, I was to be punished. They said that once the creature ate my heart, I would no longer exist. How could I no longer exist?"

"I wouldn't worry about that. If you no longer existed, you wouldn't know about it anyway," King Rhadamanthus reasoned.

"But, whether I'm in the Underworld or on the Earth, wouldn't I always exist?" Narcissus asked, confounded.

"Let's not debate existentialism, Narcissus," King Minos declared. "It won't even be invented for quite a while." Narcissus looked perplexed. "Regardless," King Minos continued, "We were having a difficult time deciding what to do with you, so, after your misadventure in Egypt, we decided to offer you a chance to better your outcome here in Hades."

"What do you mean?" Narcissus replied.

"Well, as it stands now, you could spend eternity stuck in the torture of desperately lusting after yourself, but not being able to ever physically fulfill that love."

"It's already torture!" Narcissus wailed.

"Yes," King Minos replied. "Come, Narcissus, gaze into this special mirror and tell us what you see."

Narcissus stepped forward and gazed into a circular mirror floating on the surface of a pool of water. At first, he once again saw his Beloved gazing back at him, but in moments, the image dissolved and the mirror reflection turned gray and hazy. Narcissus looked up from the mirror and toward King Minos, looking for an explanation.

"Narcissus, this is the Mirror of the Oracle, forged by the Fates. It shows the possible outcomes for your soul here in Hades. In the first of potential destinies, you can see that if you don't gain in wisdom of your Self, or learn to love another, you may be left in a hazy gray existence of nothingness."

Narcissus was upset; that was no way to spend eternity.

"Look again into the mirror," King Minos commanded.

Narcissus turned back to the mirror. In this second look, he saw his Beloved gazing at him, but instead of looking at Narcissus lovingly, the image taunted him and told him that he was ugly and unlovable. Narcissus became distraught, and he began to move away from the mirror bowl.

As he did, a third vision appeared. This time, Narcissus could see horrible and grotesque figures groping at him, declaring their undying lust for him. They then attempted to force themselves on him and he felt unable to stop their attack. Narcissus jumped back from the bowl and cried, "No! What horrors are these you're showing me?"

"They are possible eternal outcomes for you, if you do not work towards a better understanding of yourself and others," King Minos replied.

"I can't imagine experiencing any of that," Narcissus lamented. "Tell me what to do so that those fates don't become realized."

"We're going to send you on a little adventure," King Aeacus replied. "And then we shall see."

"What sort of adventure?" Narcissus asked.

"An adventure that will not only test your sense of who you really are," King Aeacus replied, "but let us know if you have what it takes."

"What it takes for what?" Narcissus asked.

"Redemption." The word hung in the air for a long moment.

"Bring him in," King Minos called out to the attendant. Narcissus heard a door open, and he turned around to see his old hunting buddy, Antagonis, standing there with an enormous grin on his face.

"Hiya, buddy!" Antagonis called out joyously in his gravelly voice. "Looks like we're going on an adventure!" Narcissus stared at Antagonis with surprise.

"Antagonis has been chosen to accompany you. He, too, has a chance to improve his fate," King Aeacus explained.

"It's good to be off the gate, King Aeacus," Antagonis interjected. "Herbie was starting to work my last nerve." King Aeacus ignored Antagonis and continued his instructions to Narcissus.

"As you go on this journey, you will have choices to make. Learn from what you see and you may just have a chance at redemption, a chance to relieve your current torment. Now on the other hand, should you prove unable to grow, unable to reflect on your projections, your doom is sealed. One of the possible outcomes you saw in the mirror bowl will become what you live in for eternity."

Narcissus shuddered when he thought about the groping hands of the ugly, grotesque figures, the cruel insults and rejection of his Beloved, and of the gray and hazy possibilities lying ahead of him.

"What would redemption look like?" Narcissus asked.

"Look into the Mirror of the Oracle again," King Aeacus instructed. Narcissus reluctantly moved back toward the bowl. He was afraid that he might see some other horror that awaited him.

Narcissus peered into the bowl and saw, to his surprise, an image of himself. He was sitting in a sunny field, enjoying a picnic of ambrosia with a young woman and a young man. Both the woman and the man looked familiar, but he couldn't place them. One thing was for sure, however, Narcissus looked happy, and he gazed lovingly, not lustfully, at the people he was with, and they, too, returned his loving expression.

8

Narcissus and Antagonis were led into a great, darkened chamber. As the lights slowly brightened, they could see that one entire wall of the chamber was covered by a massive mirror.

"Holy smokes," Antagonis cried out. "I thought I was pale, but look at you!"

Narcissus paid no attention to Antagonis; the sight in front of him - his Beloved - transfixed him. Narcissus drew in a deep breath, as did his Beloved. He gave the image a wide smile, and it again rewarded Narcissus with a mirrored reaction.

"You done admiring yourself, buddy?" Antagonis said with a smirk.

"Antagonis, please stand over to the side for a moment. This is just for Narcissus," Hermes told them.

"Oh, excuuuuuuse me!" Antagonis replied sarcastically. Then muttering under his breath, he added, "Far be it from me to stand in his spotlight."

Hermes turned toward Narcissus, "Tell me, what do you see?"

"I see my Beloved, my heart, my soul, the one person I truly love," Narcissus replied.

"What if I told you that what you see is not real?" Hermes said, quixotically.

"But he is real. He's right in front of me!" Narcissus cried.

"Yes, you see him, but he's not who you think he is."

"Then who is he?" Narcissus replied, annoyance rising.

"He is you," Hermes offered. Narcissus was growing tired of people telling him what, or who, he did and did not see, especially when they never gave him any kind of a straightforward explanation.

"Look, Narcissus, what color is his hair?"

"It's brown like mine."

"Yes, and his eyes?"

"They are a dusty blue."

"And what color eyes do you have?"

"Blue. What does any of this have to do with anything?"

"He's trying to show you something, ya dummy," came Antagonis' voice from across the room.

"Hush, Antagonis," Hermes said, as Antagonis rolled his eyes skyward. "Narcissus," Hermes continued, "everything you see in a mirror is a reflection of you. It is always only you. Everything you have ever experienced and believed is in that mirror."

Narcissus gazed at the mirror, not at all grasping what Hermes was talking about. *Maybe if I just nod and smile my warmest smile Hermes will go away,* Narcissus thought to himself. *Maybe he'll just leave me here to gaze at my love.*

Hermes could tell that Narcissus was lost in his reflection again and unable to grasp the deeper understanding he so needed to learn.

"Remember, Narcissus, everything you see in this mirror is you. Watch…" and with that, Hermes pointed his index finger toward the glass and it cracked, shattering into thousands of pieces. Narcissus looked at the mirror with shock. It was still attached to the wall, but it was now separated into numerous smaller shards, each one of them containing a different image.

"Careful, Hermes, that's seven years bad luck!" Antagonis chuckled, chiming in from the corner.

"What did you just do?" Narcissus asked, uncertain.

"I have shattered your grand illusion, but now it is up to you to discover the truth in the pieces," Hermes replied cryptically. "Look…"

Narcissus looked at the pieces of mirror. He was shocked to see one with an image of himself held in his mother's doting arms as she sang him to sleep. In another mirror shard, he watched himself as a little boy, playing by the banks of the pond. In each piece, a new image of Narcissus appeared: hunting with Antagonis and eating his first kill; floating in the river hoping to spend time with his fearsome father; treating his mother like a servant, only there to supply him with a home and food; Ameinias begging him for a moment of his time; and then Ameinias' bloody body, as it lay crumbled by Narcissus' front door; turning away from Echo, as she wept silently behind him; pushing his mother angrily during a fight about his

Beloved; and Narcissus staring into the depths of the pond, unable to move, wasting away.

Narcissus was familiar with some of the scenes and shocked by the others. There were other images, as well, that intrigued and repulsed him. In one image he saw himself, but distorted, almost as if one side of his body were falling away from him; his face contorted in grotesque mask. In another, he saw his Beloved, gazing at him steadily, breaking into a smile the moment that Narcissus smiled at him. It was all very peculiar.

"Your task, Narcissus, is to understand what these images mean and the realizations that will come with that," Hermes instructed.

"So why am I here?" Antagonis stood up and walked toward Hermes. "'Cause it looks like, once again, this is all about him!" He gestured to Narcissus. "Not that I'm ungrateful or anything. I'm happy to be off the gate! But…what's in it for me? Huh?"

"You are very important to this adventure, Antagonis," Hermes replied. "You represent Narcissus' hostility toward the world."

"I'm not hostile to anyone!" Narcissus rebuked Hermes. "I just can't be bothered by other people's needs if they get in the way of mine."

Hermes looked at Antagonis, "You serve as the voice of his antagonistic nature."

"Whoa, that's too deep for a guy from the neighborhood like me," Antagonis waved Hermes away.

"How did you die, Antagonis?" Hermes asked him bluntly.

"I was shot with a bow and arrow. The bow hit an artery in my neck, and when the arrow was taken out, I bled to death," Antagonis recalled. "It was painful as Tartarus!"

"And who was it that shot you, Antagonis?" Hermes asked.

"Narcissus did," Antagonis replied.

"That's true, but…" Narcissus began to respond.

"Yes, and how did Narcissus react afterwards?" Hermes continued.

"He told me that I had gotten in the way of his shot at a buck," Antagonis recalled.

"It was Antagonis' own fault!" Narcissus cried. "I had aimed my arrow and was just about to shoot it, when Antagonis moved two steps to the right. It was an accident!"

"It's true," Antagonis added. "I did move at the last minute. I had been standing there for ten minutes, wrestling with the buck so that it would stand still long enough for Narcissus to shoot it. I'm his stager."

"His stager?" Hermes asked.

"Yes, I stage all his prey first, get them ready for Narcissus to make the kill. I catch them and hold them in place so that he can shoot them in the heart. This time, the dumb buck moved at the last minute and Narcissus shot me instead."

"Why do you have to stage Narcissus' kills for him?" Hermes asked.

"I dunno, but all those sweet-looking nymphs would follow him around and they only looked at me when I was with him, so I did what he wanted. That was only the first part of my job, then came the portrait painting; a little known skill of mine, I might add."

"Did you resent Narcissus for what he put you through?" Hermes asked Antagonis.

"Yeah, but then I'd look at the cutie-pies watching us hunt, and I didn't care. I even de-flowered a couple of those virgins, if ya know what I mean."

"And when you were shot by Narcissus, did he get medical attention for you?"

"Not really. I told him that it wasn't a good idea to just pull the arrow out of my neck, as I could bleed to death, but Narcissus said that I looked OK. He said it just looked like a flesh wound."

"Those were very expensive arrows, Hermes," Narcissus said, attempting to defend his actions. "Rumor had it that Hephaestus himself made them before he changed careers and turned to blacksmithing. I couldn't let the doctors at Epidaurus get involved, or they would have surely cut my arrow in half to get it out of him." Before adding, "I thought he'd be fine in a couple of days."

Hermes turned back to Antagonis, "You are a part of each other's experience of the world above. In order for you both to learn and grow, you must come to see what you have projected onto each other. What beliefs about the other person made you act the way you did."

Antagonis turned back toward the shattered mirror wall and reached his hand up to the scar on his neck. Rubbing the spot where the arrow had struck, Antagonis sighed a deep sigh and said, "Can we eat first? I'm dying for a nosh…"

9

As Hermes left the chamber, he gave them some final instructions. Narcissus and Antagonis were to sit in the chamber awhile and contemplate the various mirror images. Three mirrors would call out to Narcissus. When that happened, they were both to step into the mirror, face first; then arms, then right leg, then torso, and then left leg. It seemed sort of peculiar to Antagonis, but then everything seemed peculiar to Antagonis, not to mention annoying.

As they sat and watched the images play out their lives in front of them, one of the mirrors called out Narcissus' name. He turned and stared at the mirror.

"What now?" he said to Antagonis.

"We gotta stick our faces in there," Antagonis replied.

"You first," Narcissus said.

"Oh no you don't! This is your adventure. I'm only the loveable sidekick sent along for comic relief. You stick your face in there and see what happens," Antagonis said, arms crossed in front of him.

"But what if it's something awful? At least if you go in first, then I'll know for sure," Narcissus replied.

"You really are a piece of work, ya know that? There are no sweet little nymphs around, so I don't have to do anything you say anymore," Antagonis said resolutely.

"But look at your face and look at mine. I can't risk messing up my face," Narcissus reasoned.

It was only a matter of seconds before Narcissus felt the impact on his face. Antagonis had given him a right hook to the nose with such force that Narcissus fell backwards onto the ground, shocked that anyone would have the gall to punch him.

"What did you do that for?" Narcissus wailed.

"Now you don't have to worry about what will happen to your pretty face no more," Antagonis replied. "Get up and stick your face into the mirror so we can get on with this already."

Narcissus sat up and felt his nose. It was definitely broken. He looked into one of the mirrors again and saw that his Beloved now had a broken nose as well. Narcissus looked at the mirror that had called his name and took a deep breath. Hesitating for only a moment, Narcissus plunged his face through the liquidy glass. Once through, he was amazed to see his Beloved sat there in an otherwise empty room.

"Remember the instructions Hermes gave us: face, then arms, then right leg, then torso, then left leg," Antagonis called out from the other room.

Narcissus did as he was told, for he was more intrigued that there in front of him, in what seemed like flesh and blood, was his Beloved. No mirrored reflection, as real as he was.

Narcissus quickly walked over to his Beloved and reached his arms out to embrace him, but his Beloved shook his head and said, "No." Narcissus stopped in his tracks. He had never heard his Beloved speak before, and was not sure why he wouldn't allow them to finally embrace. His Beloved gestured to a chair in front of him.

"Please, my love, sit down," the Beloved said.

Narcissus obeyed, not sure whether to believe his senses, and wondering whether this was some evil trick of his mind.

"Who are you?" Narcissus asked, now unsure.

"I'm a part of you, Narcissus. The part that always tells you the truth, no matter whether you wish to hear it or not," the Beloved replied.

"OK..." Narcissus said, not entirely understanding.

"There is a part in all of us that always speaks the truth. It understands the deepest wisdom, even though we may choose to, or not to, pay attention to it," said the Beloved.

"You mean like a conscience?" Narcissus asked. He had heard about such a thing before, but had dismissed it as nonsense.

"Different. I'm not a judge of right or wrong behavior, just what's true and not true," the Beloved replied.

"So what's true?" Narcissus asked.

"I'm here to explain why you can never have me, not in the way that you want to," the Beloved replied.

"But you want me too, don't you? Every time I reached for you, you reached back as well. When I spoke words of love to you, I saw you mouth those words in return," Narcissus cried.

"Narcissus, when you look at me, you are only seeing yourself. In fact, any time you see someone, you are really only seeing yourself."

"What do you mean? Other people don't look like me," Narcissus said nonplussed.

"No they don't, but *how* you see them comes from within you. The only reason why I look like you is because you've been cursed to desperately love yourself and only yourself."

"But why? I know I've been under some kind of spell, but a *curse*? Who would curse me? And why?" Narcissus could not believe that anyone would hate him enough to curse him.

It was then that he remembered Ameinias' note. He had said that he'd asked the gods to curse him.

"Ameinias! He's the one. How could he do that to me?" Narcissus cried.

"It was Ameinias' broken heart that cried out, but it was Nemesis who applied the curse. You needed to learn a lesson; a lesson that obviously you still have yet to learn," the Beloved replied.

"How do I break this curse? If what you're telling me is true, then how do I make it stop? How do I stop loving you…err…myself?"

"Narcissus, it's possible to still love yourself, but it's a different kind of love than you've expressed towards me," the Beloved continued. "It's a love that also includes loving other people."

"Other people?" Narcissus retorted.

Just then, Antagonis' face popped through the mirror in the wall.

"Hey, buddy, all safe in here? Is the coast clear?" Antagonis noticed the two Narcissuses sitting on chairs facing each other. "Whoa! What the…I'm seeing double!" And with that, his face quickly withdrew from the wall. Narcissus and his Beloved were alone once again.

Narcissus turned back to his Beloved and said, "Antagonis was a sufficient hunting buddy, but he's well annoying. I can't believe he interrupted us! What was he thinking?"

"Narcissus, what do you think about how you treat other people?" the Beloved asked.

"What do you mean?" Narcissus asked.

"Do you ever try to understand them and what they may want and need?"

"I have no idea what you're talking about. What does it matter what they want or need?"

"That is precisely the issue, Narcissus," the Beloved replied. "To truly love another, you must be able to consider their feelings and feel compassion for their needs, as well as your own."

"Give me an example," Narcissus said indignantly.

"OK, Echo, why did you treat her so cruelly when all she wanted was to embrace you?"

"That girl followed me everywhere and she had that annoying habit of repeating everything I said. What was wrong with her?" Narcissus said.

"She was cursed, Narcissus, just like you. Her curse was different, though. She used to talk very freely, until one day she stopped Hera along the road and gossiped with her for hours in order to delay her from finding her husband, Zeus, in a compromising position with a river nymph. Hera was so mad at Echo for protecting Zeus, that she cursed her to only repeat the last words that anyone said in her presence."

"Oh," Narcissus replied. "I didn't know that."

"If you had, would that have changed how you treated her?" the Beloved asked. Narcissus thought for a moment.

"She still tried to embrace me when I didn't want her to," Narcissus said.

"Yes, that may be, but she did have feelings for you, and so may have misunderstood your initial response to her," the Beloved replied. "But rather than explain to her that you didn't have the same feelings, you called her a wretched creature and turned your back on her. How would you have felt if I had done that to you?"

"It would have been awful," Narcissus admitted. "But that's hardly reason enough to be cursed!"

"Well, and then there's Ameinias. He waited for you every day, and when he told you he couldn't live without you, you basically told him to kill himself."

"I did no such thing. I just told him to leave me alone and gave him a sword."

"Yes, you gave a depressed and heartbroken young man a sharp sword, as you told him that his love would never be requited. What did you think might happen?" the Beloved inquired.

"I'm not responsible for his death! He chose to do that!" Narcissus growled, his temper rising.

"True, it was his choice, but your callousness and indifference have consequences. Your behavior affects other people."

Narcissus sat quietly and thought about what his Beloved had said. He looked deeply into the Beloved's eyes, and felt love surge through his body stronger than ever before. He did love this man, and he considered if what he had been saying was indeed true.

"How many people, Narcissus, have loved you in your lifetime?" the Beloved asked.

"Well, my mother and maybe my father, the young women and men in the village, some demi-goddesses, Dionysus, some visiting merchants from the outlying villages, the nymphs, a few of the muses, you…"

"And of all of those, Narcissus, how many have you loved?"

Narcissus shrugged his shoulders, "I love my mother. I'm supposed to love her, right? She's my mother. And you, of course, I love you most of all."

"Don't you think that's odd? That the only people you've ever loved are me, your own reflection, and your mother, who you feel obligated to love?" the Beloved asked.

"I think I understand what you are trying to tell me," Narcissus responded.

"Do you? Do you understand it, or do you realize it? They are very different things," replied the Beloved.

"I understand what you're telling me; that I should pay more attention to other people and their feelings. And that maybe I should consider that others may be worthy of my love as well."

"Good," the Beloved said.

Exhaling deeply, Narcissus asked, "So now what? Am I done with my adventure? Did I learn what I needed to and they'll remove the curse? Or can we be together for real now?"

"Not quite yet, Narcissus," the Beloved replied. "You still have more to learn." Narcissus frowned, disappointed that there was more he'd have to do. "Go back through the mirror and wait for another mirror shard to call to you." The Beloved rose from his chair and Narcissus stood up as well.

"Can I at least embrace you while we're here in this room together?" Narcissus asked hopefully.

"No, Narcissus," the Beloved replied gently, "The time will come when we will merge together in love, but not yet." He pointed to the mirror on the wall through which Narcissus had come. "Go now, my love."

"I do love you, my Beloved," Narcissus said as he stepped through the mirror.

"I love you too," the Beloved replied, as Narcissus disappeared from the room.

10

As Narcissus returned to the room with the shattered mirror, he saw Antagonis perched in front of one long sliver of glass on the far end of the room. He was making faces into the glass, and laughing uproariously at his facial contortions.

"What are you doing?" Narcissus asked him.

"Oh hiya, buddy, I was just having fun. Look at this face! Ya know, when I was little, my mother told me that if I kept making funny faces, my face would freeze that way," Antagonis chuckled.

"Well, she was right, obviously" Narcissus said matter-of-factly, gesturing toward Antagonis.

"Hey!" Antagonis complained. "So where's the second Narcissus? The one you were talking to. What was that all about?"

"He was my Beloved," Narcissus sighed. "I was finally able to properly talk with him, but he was only there to tell me some things he said that I needed to hear."

"Like what?" Antagonis asked, now curious.

Narcissus paused silently for a moment. He wasn't sure that he wanted to share it all with Antagonis quite yet. There was still so much for him to think about.

"Apparently," Narcissus began, "I haven't treated people all that nicely in the past."

"Ya don't say," Antagonis said sarcastically. "And 'in the past?' So does that mean that you will start treating people nicely now?"

"Well, I'll certainly be more aware of what I say, but tell me Antagonis, haven't I always treated you nice enough?"

Antagonis reached up to rub his neck scar, and said, "You want the real answer or the 'Narcissus' answer?"

Just as Narcissus began to reply, the mirror that Antagonis was sitting in front of began to call Narcissus' name.

"Hey, this one's calling for you!" Antagonis said. "Should I come with you this time?"

Narcissus was about to say "no," as he was tiring of Antagonis' caustic remarks. But, as he contemplated what his Beloved had said to him, he found himself deciding to invite Antagonis along. *Who knows? Maybe he'll come in handy in there,* Narcissus thought to himself.

He walked over to the mirror and gazed in it. In this one, everything seemed to be somehow warped. The image of his Beloved could be seen in the glass, an image Narcissus now knew to also be himself, but the reflection was warped slightly, and his face and body looked distorted. The mirror called his name again, and so with a deep breath, Narcissus plunged his face into the fluid glass.

11

Narcissus entered the new room, followed closely by Antagonis.

"Whoa! Trippy!' Antagonis cried out, bemused. Everything in the room looked distorted, almost as if it was a funhouse. A putrid smell arose from the corners of the room, as they noticed rotting food and feces smeared liberally about. Both men recoiled from the smell and looked at each other questioningly.

"OK, that's putrid," Antagonis said, "I'm outta here!" And as they both turned to exit the room through the mirror from which they had come, two men appeared, blocking their exit. Narcissus and Antagonis both drew back in disgust. The two men looked like strange warped versions of themselves. Antagonis' strange double had tiny little arms and hands, no bigger than 5 inches in length protruding from his full sized body, and to Antagonis' horror, he had no mouth. Only skin was present where a mouth should be.

"Oh my Zeus! Oh my Hades!" Antagonis cried.

Narcissus stood immobile in front of his own double. He was frozen in shock, trying his best to assimilate what he was seeing. Somehow, he still knew that this was both his Beloved and himself, but the love and longing he couldn't help but feel for this disturbing figure troubled him even more than he could say.

"Narcissus!" his double shrieked at him. "You wretched creature! I could never truly love anyone as horribly ugly as you!"

Narcissus was dumbfounded. *I'm ugly?* It was his Beloved who now appeared ugly. *And what did he mean that he could never truly love me?*

"How could you not love me?" Narcissus asked. "Are you not the same Beloved I just spoke to, who declared he loved me too?"

"I am another version of your Beloved. And I only love those who are as beautiful as myself," his double replied.

"But you're horrid!" cried Narcissus.

"No, it is you who are horrid, prancing around like you're perfect. Looking down your nose at everyone. You disgust me!"

Narcissus was so confused. This version of his Beloved looked dirty and unkempt, and slightly warped, and the way he was speaking to Narcissus shocked him. And yet,

Narcissus still loved him so, forced by the curse to recognize and long for him.

"I do still love you, Beloved," Narcissus cried, and attempted to reach his arms out to the horrible figure.

"Get away from me! Don't touch me!" his double replied. Narcissus felt heartbroken. Why would his Beloved recoil at his touch?

Narcissus sat down on the ground and wept. *What do I do now? My only love has rejected me.*

Meanwhile, on the other side of the room, Antagonis' double was poking and prodding at him, and making horrible noises from its throat. The skin over where his mouth should be, stretched in response. Antagonis' double then picked up a fireplace poker and began chasing Antagonis around the room.

"Stop! What are you doing?" Antagonis cried. But the double would not respond, he would only mock Antagonis with a guttural noise and continue to prod him with the poker.

"We gotta get outta here," Antagonis called over to Narcissus. For the first time, Antagonis noticed that Narcissus was crumpled on the ground, crying.

"My Beloved doesn't love me anymore," Narcissus said through muffled cries.

"You should be grateful of that! Come on." Antagonis grabbed Narcissus' arm, but he wouldn't move.

"Ya still want me, you abominable wretch?" Narcissus' double called out menacingly. "Come here and I'll give you what you want."

Narcissus looked up into the face of his Beloved. Even though it was not the face he was used to seeing, he could not stop himself from longing to be held by him. Narcissus reached his arms up toward the warped double, and looked hopefully into his eyes. Rather than the gentle touch Narcissus had hoped for, this version of his Beloved grabbed a hold of Narcissus and pushed him backwards onto the floor. Narcissus was not sure what to do. He was not used to being treated so roughly. This Beloved roughly flipped Narcissus over and began to rip at his clothes. *This was not what I wanted*, Narcissus thought to himself desperately.

"Say it, Narcissus! Say that you want me!" his double growled at him, as he brutally grabbed a hold of Narcissus' body.

Narcissus cried out with all the strength he had, "Stop, please stop! I don't want this!"

Before Narcissus or his Beloved's warped double could say another word, Antagonis rushed over to Narcissus and yanked him out from underneath the monster. Half dragging and half carrying, he threw himself and Narcissus through the mirror in the wall and returned to the room with the shattered mirror. They were both breathing rapidly and erratically; Narcissus crumpled into a fetal position on the floor, sobbing uncontrollably.

"Don't say it, Antagonis," Narcissus wailed. "Don't say that I deserved that. I was never that horrible. No one deserves that!"

Antagonis reached over to Narcissus and threw an arm comfortingly around him. "You're right, my friend," Antagonis said gently, himself still shaken. "You didn't deserve that. No one does. You're safe now, Narcissus." And the two men huddled there for some time before either one of them felt able to move again.

12

After what felt like a long while, Narcissus raised his head and looked Antagonis in the eyes.

"Antagonis…" he began.

"Yeah, buddy?" Antagonis replied.

"Remember what Hermes said to us?"

"When?"

"Before he shattered the mirror. He said that everything I see in the mirror is me," Narcissus said with concern. "So that awful man…was me?"

Antagonis paused for a moment, and thought about it. He, too, had experienced an awful version of himself in that mirror. *What did it mean?* he thought to himself.

"I think yes and no," Antagonis replied after some contemplation. "I think that, as Hermes said, it may be a part of us, that awful part, but it's not all of who we are. It's only one part."

"It was horrible," Narcissus whispered.

"Yeah," Antagonis responded, "I guess we all have a monster in us. We just don't always get a chance to see it in action." Antagonis began to remember all the times that he had intentionally annoyed those around him, friends, family, and strangers alike. He hadn't really cared about whether it bothered them, or whether they had felt terrorized and mistreated. Maybe it was time he reconsidered things.

"So what were my crimes?" Narcissus asked him. "I never forced myself on anyone. I never physically attacked anyone. How could that be the monster in me?"

"I don't know, Narcissus," Antagonis responded. "But your disregard for others' feelings and needs was pretty bad. People died because you cared so little for them. Your needs and desires came before everyone else's. Maybe that's it."

Narcissus stood up and began pacing the room.

"I never asked for any of them to love me. I didn't mean to be brutal about it, I just didn't want to be bothered. I guess, when I saw my Beloved for the first time, I felt differently." Turning back toward Antagonis, Narcissus asked, "What else have I done that was monstrous?"

Antagonis looked at Narcissus, "Umm…well…a lot. Sorry, buddy." Normally, this would have been the fun part for Antagonis, pointing out someone's flaws and pushing their buttons, but since his experience in the last mirror, he felt no desire to cause anyone else pain. He looked up at Narcissus, who looked apprehensive.

"Well," Antagonis began gently, "Often you would treat people like they didn't matter, and that we were just there to participate in your life, as you needed us. You didn't much care for our feelings or needs, or even if your actions would cause us pain. Or in my case, even death."

As Antagonis reached up to touch his neck, Narcissus saw the scar clearly for the first time.

"But I never intended to cause anyone harm. I definitely didn't mean for the arrow to hit you."

"I know, buddy, but that's just it. Your indifference to others can turn out harmful, just the same as if you'd intended them harm."

Just then, a third mirror called out to Narcissus. Both men turned to look into it, now wary about what they might find there. It was a loving image of Narcissus' Beloved, but after the last experience, neither man made a move toward it.

"I don't think I'm ready for another mirror," Narcissus said.

"I know what'cha mean," Antagonis replied.

As they stood there staring at the mirror, a new image appeared in it. It was another image of Narcissus, walking toward the Beloved. Reaching out his arms, the Beloved embraced "Mirror Narcissus" and they held one another tenderly. Watching all of this unfold, Narcissus, still in the room with Antagonis, was mesmerized.

Narcissus continued to watch as the two images of himself frolicked in the meadow, made love under the stars at night, and strolled happily through the village. Narcissus felt a strong desire to join them in the mirror.

"I've decided to enter this mirror, Antagonis. Do you want to come along too?"

"No, buddy, I think I'll stay here and let you have some time with your Beloved, um…Beloveds…alone. It looks very loving in that mirror, Narcissus."

"Yes," Narcissus agreed, his eyes tearing up. "It's what I desire most of all."

13

Narcissus stepped into the mirror and found himself face to face with himself and his Beloved. They both turned to smile at him, and the Mirror Narcissus walked toward him and, much to Narcissus' amazement, dissolved into Narcissus' own body. Narcissus was now that version of himself. The Beloved smiled at Narcissus just as lovingly as he had at the Mirror Narcissus, and they held hands and walked through the woods together.

Narcissus had never felt this happy before. For the first time, he felt truly loved, truly seen, and truly alive. As he and his Beloved reached a large tree stump, they sat down and ate the picnic lunch that had been waiting next to the stump.

While they were eating, a tiny bird hopped tentatively up to their meal. Narcissus' first instinct was to swat it away, as he didn't want to it ruin their idyllic picnic. But as Narcissus raised his hand toward the bird, the Beloved stopped him.

"Look, Narcissus, she has a broken wing. We have enough food for her as well, my love," the Beloved said sweetly. He held a morsel of bread in the palm of his hand and gently offered it to the little bird. The bird moved its head up to look at the Beloved and make sure that it was safe, and then slowly hopped closer to the open hand, gratefully pecking at the bread. Narcissus watched as his Beloved gently hand-fed the little bird until the bird was full. He felt a rush of love well up in him; such as he had never known. He loved his Beloved so much. He loved how tender and generous he was.

Suddenly, Narcissus remembered what Hermes had said: "Everyone you see in the mirror is you." *Could that be?* Narcissus wondered. *Could this Beloved, this tender loving Beloved, be me as well?*

The little bird, now satisfied, began to chirp a beautiful tune. In response, a chorus of tiny chirps could be heard. Narcissus and his beloved looked up into the tree and found a nest filled with even smaller baby birds.

"This momma bird can't fly back up to the nest, so she can't feed her young. Let's help them," the Beloved stood up and began to climb the tree.

"Wait!" Narcissus cried. "Let me, I don't want you to fall."

The Beloved smiled at Narcissus, "Thank you, my love. I'll stand here and you can hand the nest down to me."

Narcissus climbed nimbly up the tree and reached the bird nest. There were three baby birds in the nest chirping at him and flapping their not-ready-for-flying wings.

Narcissus knew that in the past, he would never have risked harming himself to climb a tree and save birds. They were just birds, after all. But this time, it seemed like the right thing to do. Plus, it meant a lot to his Beloved and so it meant a lot to him as well. Carefully extracting the nest from the tree branch it rested on, Narcissus climbed partially down the tree and then handed the nest over to his Beloved. The Beloved then brought the nest over to their picnic area, where the mother bird waited anxiously.

Narcissus jumped down the rest of the way to the ground and joined them over by the tree stump. They both tore off small pieces of bread and handed it to the baby birds, but the baby birds couldn't eat them. The mother bird then hopped over and took the bread from out of Narcissus' hand.

"That's terrible!" Narcissus exclaimed. "After all that, she won't let us feed her babies! She's only thinking of herself, I don't believe it!"

"No, my love," the Beloved explained, "She's right, how silly of us. Look!"

The mother bird chewed on the bread until it was soft and wet, and then hopped over to the baby birds and offered the bread from her mouth to theirs.

"Oh!" Narcissus exclaimed, and immediately he thought of his own mother, Liriope. *I was a baby once*, he thought, *obviously she didn't need to feed me that way, but in what other ways did she care for me?* Narcissus felt a pang of remorse for how he had treated his mother. She had always been there for him, not matter what. He wished that she would walk into this mirror world so he could tell her that he loved her. Narcissus looked back at the mother bird and saw that she had dug up some worms, which she was now busy chewing up to feed to her little ones.

When the birds were done eating, they all chirped happily. But Narcissus noticed that the mother bird could not hop back into the nest, as she couldn't fly and the edge of the nest was too high for her. Without thinking, he reached over and gently offered his hand out to her. She hopped onto it and Narcissus placed her in the nest next to her babies. He smiled to himself, seeing them all together and happy.

Narcissus glanced up at his Beloved, who was gazing lovingly at him.

"What happens to them now?" Narcissus asked. "I know these woods, and it won't be long before a wild boar or wolf comes by. They won't stand a chance."

"You're right," the beloved responded, thoughtfully. "Let's take them with us and nurse the mother bird's wing back to health. Then when she's healed, we can return them to the woods."

Narcissus agreed, and as he and his Beloved walked back to the village, Narcissus was again struck with the notion that everything in his life was exactly as he desired it to be. He sighed contentedly.

When they reached the home that they shared, Narcissus remembered the last mirror world and the horrible, warped Beloved he had encountered. A troubled look came over his face.

Noticing the look, his Beloved asked, "What is it, my love? What's the matter?"

Narcissus sat down and began to explain what had happened to him in the other mirror world. He felt his body shake again, simply by the memory.

When he had finished, Narcissus looked at his Beloved and saw that he was nodding.

"Yes, I know about him," the Beloved responded.

"But how?" Narcissus asked, shocked.

"He's your shadow, as am I. We're part of you, and you are part of us."

Narcissus was nonplussed, "That's what Hermes told me."

"Well, he should know!" the Beloved said, laughing. "He's hangs out in the space between the shadows and the Self."

Narcissus rubbed his forehead, as though nursing a headache, "What doesn't make sense to me is how I can be all of these different people. I never saw myself as any of these other versions."

"Yes, it's amazing how a little thing like a mirrored glass can show you so much more than you ever thought possible," the Beloved said, smiling.

"But how could you love me, knowing that somewhere in me is also that monster?" Narcissus asked imploringly. "How could you love a monster?"

"I love you, Narcissus," the Beloved said reassuringly. "I love all of who you are. I can see the gentle, loving, and thoughtful side of you, but the more *you* can see the many parts of you, the more full and happy you'll be, and the more full our relationship can be. Just because you also have a part of you that feels a disconnection and disregard for others' feelings, does not mean that it has to become who you are. Seeing all of it, embracing all of it, and watching how you react to the people and things around you will make you the whole and happy Narcissus that I *know* you can be!"

The Beloved reached his hand out to Narcissus, gently pulling him closer to him. Narcissus embraced him and rested his head on his Beloved's strong shoulder. For the first time in his entire life, Narcissus felt whole.

14

"It's time to go now, Narcissus." Narcissus turned his head to look at the voice, and saw that it was Hermes entering his house. Releasing his Beloved's embrace, Narcissus turned to face Hermes and greeted him.

"Thank you for all you've taught me, Hermes. I've learned so much," Narcissus began. "But, everything seems so perfect here, why can't I stay here in this mirror with my Beloved. He's shown me things about myself I've never known possible."

"Yes you have, Narcissus, but there is still another magic mirror you must see," Hermes replied.

"But you said there were only three?" Narcissus said imploringly. "This is the third. I'm done, right?"

"There were three that called out to you, that's true. But I have one more very important one for you look in."

Narcissus turned to his Beloved, upset at the thought of parting from him once again.

"Narcissus," the Beloved said. "I am a part of you, so we can never truly be apart. We've been able to physically embrace here, that's true, and that's been beautiful. But, if you stop for a moment and feel the love in your heart, you'll be feeling me. That's where I live when I'm not in this mirror world." The Beloved gestured to the room around him.

"I'll love you forever, my Beloved," Narcissus cried and ran into his Beloved's arms.

"Indeed, forever, my love," the Beloved responded. "How can we ever truly be separated?"

"Come now, Narcissus," Hermes urged.

Narcissus released his Beloved and followed Hermes toward the pedestaled dressing mirror at the far corner of the room. Taking one last glance at his Beloved and the nest of birds they had been caring for, Narcissus stepped through the mirror and back into the shattered mirror room.

15

"Hey, buddy!" Antagonis greeted him, as he stepped back into the room.

"Hi, Antagonis," Narcissus replied. "That was such a different experience than the last one! It was so beautiful and loving."

"I'm so glad," he replied. As Narcissus was about to relay all of the wonderful experiences he had had, he stopped himself and decided to ask Antagonis what he had been doing while he waited.

"How are you doing? Did anything happen for you while I was away?" Narcissus inquired.

Taken aback by Narcissus' interest in his wellbeing, Antagonis replied, "Nothing really, I just had some quiet time to think about a lot of things."

"Do you want to talk about it?" Narcissus asked, surprised at himself for even caring if Antagonis needed to talk.

"Thanks, buddy, but I'm good," Antagonis replied, with a big warm smile.

"Come stand over here, Narcissus," Hermes requested.

Narcissus walked over and stood next to Hermes. They were in front of a big chunk of mirror on the shattered wall. In the mirrored reflection, Narcissus once again saw his Beloved.

"This piece of mirror," Hermes began, "will show you some of the people in your life who you've met; some you've hurt, some you've simply ignored. Look now, Narcissus, the image you see is of Echo, the young nymph you insulted and turned away from."

Narcissus looked deeper into the mirror image. Still, he only saw his Beloved. In this image, however, his Beloved was following him and crying, dejected. Narcissus looked at Hermes, confused.

"But that's not Echo, that's my Beloved," Narcissus said.

"No, that's Echo," Hermes insisted.

Narcissus looked at the image again, willing himself to see what Hermes could see. But still, he only saw his Beloved.

"I don't understand. I see my Beloved and I love him, but why would he be crying as if I had turned away from him?"

"Because it is Echo you're seeing in the mirror," Hermes responded.

Narcissus didn't want to look like a fool in front of Hermes, so he decided to tell the god what he wanted to hear, "Oh, yes, I see her now. I see Echo."

"That's good, Narcissus," said Hermes, knowing full well that Narcissus had only seen himself in the mirror. This test would be one of the most important tests of all for Narcissus.

"OK, Narcissus, look again into the mirror, I will now show you Ameinias," Hermes said.

Narcissus looked into the mirror, but once again, he only saw his Beloved and felt pure love for the image. The Beloved in the mirror was down on hands and knees begging for Narcissus' love.

"But you have my love, Beloved!" Narcissus cried out.

"Ameinias never had your love, Narcissus," Hermes rebuked him.

Narcissus looked back into the mirror again, knowing that even though Hermes said that he should be seeing Ameinias, all he could see was his own Beloved."

"Oh, yes, that's true," Narcissus responded, trying to appease Hermes.

In the next moment, to his horror, the Beloved in the mirror took the sword that had belonged to Narcissus and plunged it deeply into his own heart.

"*No!*" cried Narcissus, attempting to step through the mirror, but this mirror was only a mirror, and not a portal like the others. "*Stop!*" he cried, banging his hands against the glass in protest. Hoping beyond hope that his Beloved would hear him and that he could be saved in time.

"You cannot stop Ameinias from taking his own life, as this event has already occurred. It is your history. Ameinias is now here in Hades," Hermes told him.

Narcissus watched as the crumpled body of his Beloved lay there in the doorway, and to further his horror, an image of himself appeared, bent down, withdrew the sword from the Beloved's body, and walked off to the brook to wash it off, leaving the bloody body to writhe in its final death throes. Narcissus fell to his knees and sobbed with long heaving cries.

After a few minutes, Hermes said, "Stand up now, Narcissus. There is another image to show you. Your mother, Liriope."

Narcissus stood up and was surprised to again see his Beloved standing there, smiling lovingly at him. He felt the pangs of longing in him for this shining face.

"But that, surely, is not my mother, as I desire this vision in the mirror. I have no such desire for my mother!" Narcissus cried out.

"But it is, Narcissus. That is the very image of your mother," Hermes replied.

Narcissus watched as his Beloved cooked for him and washed his clothes. He watched as he sat alone by the hearth busily tending to Narcissus' every need. He watched as he sat alone at the table waiting for his son to come home, and he watched as he neglected his own needs so that he would be available to tend to his. And finally, Narcissus saw himself push his Beloved away from himself at the pond's edge, hurtling him backwards onto the ground. He watched as his Beloved arose, injured and crying.

"Yes, it must be," Narcissus began, "but…" He was unable to continue, as he couldn't reconcile the desire he felt for the image of his Beloved with this view of his mother.

"The reason you still feel uncontrollable desire for the images you see, is because of the curse," Hermes explained. "You are still under Nemesis' curse. But, by being able to see your Beloved in everyone, there is still hope for your redemption. Remember what I said to you earlier, everyone you see in your world is a reflection of you. Treat them all as you would your Beloved."

"But I don't want to feel desire for everyone I see," Narcissus responded, confused.

"Yes, you're right. Love is the pure feeling; care for and have compassion for others as if they were your own Beloved, because in a way, they are. How you treat others, and how you treat yourself are directly related to each other. The parts of you that feel anger and apathy, and the parts of you that feel love and compassion are all you. The others in your life experience those things as well. How you interact with them is determined by which parts of yourself you are aware of, and whether you understand each part's needs."

Narcissus stood, deep in thought for a moment.

"You know, Hermes," Antagonis interrupted. "Until recently, I would have made fun of all that psycho-babble! 'Parts of us and so on…' But I get it now."

"Yes, so do I," Narcissus said thoughtfully. "It never occurred to me that how I viewed other people in my life like Echo, Ameinias, my mother, all came out of me. They were only annoying because of the monster part of me, the part that didn't think anyone else's needs and desires were important. But now I realize that there is more to me. I have a compassion part too. One that had almost been totally forgotten."

"Well done, Narcissus. Then it's time," Hermes announced.

"Time for what?" Narcissus asked.

"To meet Persephone."

16

Hermes, Narcissus, and Antagonis left the chamber with the shattered mirror on the wall, and found themselves walking through a field of black flowers.

"I thought nothing could grow here in Hades," Narcissus asked Hermes.

"That's mostly true, but flowers can grow in only two places in the Underworld, here and in the Elysian Fields. This is Persephone's garden. When Persephone found out that she was to be Queen of the Underworld for half the year, she wept and wept. Hades asked her if there was anything he could do to make her stay happier here, and she said that besides her mother, she missed seeing flowers the most. So Hades had this garden planted for her."

"Flowers without sunlight?" Antagonis mused. "Far out!"

"In reality, anything is possible, even here," Hermes replied.

Narcissus looked up at the large and magnificent castle they were approaching. It was made of black lava rock, with turrets of shiny obsidian, though the curtains were a surprising lavender lace.

"You should have seen it before!" Hermes smiled. "It definitely needed a lady's touch."

As they entered the castle's Great Hall, they saw Persephone sitting on one of the two ornate thrones at the far end of the room. The other throne, belonging to Hades, was empty.

"Whew," Antagonis sighed with relief. "I have to admit, I was a little afraid of meeting Hades in person." Narcissus nodded his agreement.

"Greetings, Queen Persephone!" Hermes called out.

"Hello, dear brother. Thank you for bringing them to me."

"Of course," he replied with a twinkle in his eye. "Will you be needing me any more today?"

"No," Persephone smiled. "Oh, but will you do me a favor please, Hermes? Will you tell my mother that I love her and bring her this pretty ring I had fashioned from the obsidian rock I found in my garden?"

"Absolutely," Hermes said, reaching for the ring.

As he slipped the ring onto one of his own fingers, Persephone added, "And Hermes, make sure you actually give the ring to my mother, and don't sell it this time, OK?"

"Yes, of course," Hermes responded with a faux shocked expression.

"I mean it, Hermes!" Persephone again implored.

"Yes, dearest Persephone," he said with a mischievous glint in his eye; and off he went in a gust of wind.

Persephone turned to the handmaiden next to her, and said doubtfully, "You think my mother will actually get this one?"

Her handmaiden smiled encouragingly, "It's possible."

Persephone turned back to Narcissus and Antagonis, who had been waiting patiently.

"Do you know why you are here?" she asked.

"All that Hermes said was that it was time for me to meet you," Narcissus responded.

"Yes, that's right. You have been working very hard on yourself since you've arrived in Hades; more so than the judges believed you would. Because of that, I want to give you an opportunity to free yourself of Nemesis' curse. I wish to show you one last image. Please come forward, Narcissus," Persephone motioned for him to step toward her. "This bowl is a clear reflection of you and your life thus far. There are no projections, and no false images. Simply look into it and tell me what you see."

Narcissus peered into this bowl of water and was amazed to see himself looking back at him. It was not his Beloved, but himself smiling back at him. This image quickly dissolved, and in its place, Narcissus could see the day he was born. He watched as his mother lovingly held him in her arms, soothing his cries, and nursing him tenderly. He felt a rush of pure love for his mother, the one person who had always been there for him, no matter what he had said or done. He watched as his childhood played out, how he went from innocent baby to self-involved young man, ignoring the attentions of others and disregarding their feelings as meaningless.

Narcissus felt compassion for the people he had hurt, but more surprisingly, he felt compassion for his young self. He realized that the great wounds he had suffered in his relationship with his River God father had turned into a lack of care for others. His father had left Narcissus' mother after their one savage encounter and gone on to live his life elsewhere, roaring down one river or another. Narcissus saw that his desire to be worthy of his distant and malicious father's love, and his inability to understand why his father didn't seem to want to know him, had caused him to disconnect from those who did care about him. Narcissus, at once, felt ashamed of himself, but he also felt great love for that little boy and the pain he had experienced. He watched as year after year, his inability to feel love and be loved grew until he was no longer able to care for anyone.

Narcissus watched as his mother tended to his every need, and yet he disregarded her, treating her as his servant; never fully appreciating her love.

He watched as he accidentally shot Antagonis, and callously blamed his hunting partner for the fatal wounding. He watched as Antagonis died in agony, bleeding out because Narcissus didn't feel like going to get medical help. He watched as he walked away, disconnected from feelings and from the world.

Narcissus looked up from the bowl and looked at Antagonis standing to the side of him.

With tears in his eyes, Narcissus said, "I truly am sorry, my friend. I should have been more careful and I should have tried to get you help after it happened."

"I know, buddy," Antagonis said, appreciating Narcissus' remorse. "It's OK."

Narcissus turned back to the bowl and watched as Echo had attempted to connect with him, offering him her love and companionship. He watched as he had ignored her, and as he had taken his anger out on her. But he cried for her broken heart, and for how his inability to love had harmed both of them.

He watched as Ameinias waited for him day after day, and saw the forlorn look on his face when Narcissus slammed the door in his face. Again, Narcissus felt his heart grow, as he felt love for both Ameinias and this wounded Narcissus, who couldn't understand that his own unrealized pain was causing others such grief.

Narcissus saw the beauty in all of it, in the love and in the pain, and felt overcome. He watched as Nemesis cursed him, and as he lay by the water, unable to leave his own reflection. He watched as his mother attempted to reason with him and bring him home, and how he felt that he had finally found that perfect love; not realizing that he had been looking for the love of his father, the lack of which had caused him to shut out all others.

He saw his image in the water, as it reflected back every movement, every sigh, and realized that all of the pain he had felt, all of the protections he had placed on his heart, had melted away. Gratitude filled Narcissus, as he had been given this opportunity to see his life for what it really was, to see himself and others as they truly were, rather than through the lens of his pain.

Narcissus glanced up at Persephone and saw how beautiful she was. He sank down to his knees and thanked her for this experience.

"Dearest Queen Persephone, I have never felt this much love before. It's not desire or longing, just pure love for myself, for everyone. How can I ever repay you enough for this?" Narcissus cried out.

"Why would you need to repay me? All I have done is show you who you truly are. You have always been that, it's just that sometimes we need to look in the mirrors we have around us, in order to truly see ourselves. You've done well, Narcissus! Because of that, I have lifted Nemesis' curse. If you continue to look carefully at those around you, you may still be able to see them as if they were your Beloved."

"Thank you, Queen Persephone! I am so thankful."

"And you, Antagonis," Persephone turned toward him. "You have been very patiently waiting during this time, and I want to tell you that I am very pleased with your progress as well." Antagonis smiled in appreciation. "You also needed to learn compassion, though your wounds were different. Rather than make things more unpleasant for Narcissus, you comforted him when you, too, were upset. This shows how much you have grown.

"So now, Narcissus, we come to the final decision on where in Hades you shall remain for eternity. I have been consulting with King Minos, and we have decided to let you choose where you are to go." Narcissus looked at Persephone with surprise.

After a moment's reflection, he responded, "I would very much like to see Ameinias and Echo and have a chance to tell them how sorry I am, and that I should have been much kinder to them."

"Very well," Persephone said with a smile. "Ameinias is in the Asphodel Fields, wandering in the area behind this castle. You may go to him and make your peace, then continue on to the Elysian Fields, where you will find Echo. After that, should you choose to, you may remain in Elysium, or you may return here, as you wish."

"Thank you, Queen Persephone," Narcissus responded.

"Antagonis," Persephone continued. "I assume that you'd prefer not to return to the gate," she said with a smile.

"I would love to stay here in Hades, rather than hang on that gate again, that's true. It really killed my back, that gate!"

"Then feel free to remain here in Hades, Antagonis," Persephone replied.

"Umm…one question though, Queen Persephone," Antagonis began tentatively.

"Yes?"

"It's just that, well, I feel sorry for Herbie, umm I mean Herbavoris. He's still stuck there on the door, and though he annoyed the crap outta me… oh, excuse me Your Highness, but he could be really trying at times. I'd love to at least offer him some hope, as you've so graciously offered me."

Persephone stayed silent for a moment, contemplating Antagonis' request.

"Do you know why Herbavoris is on the gate?" she asked him.

"No," Antagonis admitted. "He never said."

"He picked a large handful of my beautiful black flowers, and then attempted to smoke them! They are the only flowers I can grow down here and he decided to smoke them!"

"Oh, Herbie…" Antagonis shook his head. "He was always a little funny that way…"

"Nevertheless, you may return to the gate as you wish and spend time with him, should you choose to."

"I don't have to get back on the gate if I visit him?" Antagonis asked, horrified at the thought.

"No, you have earned your freedom. And you may tell Herbavoris that he may leave the gate under one condition: that he become my gardener, and tend my flower garden. However, should he destroy any of them, or attempt to smoke them, he will return to the door immediately. Understood?"

"Yes, Queen Persephone, I'll tell him!" Antagonis said, excitedly. He was happy to do a good deed, even if he wasn't too sure that Herbavoris would be able to handle the generous challenge being offered to him.

"Good. Now go, both of you. I am very pleased."

Narcissus and Antagonis bowed to Persephone and hurried out of the castle. Once outside, they stopped and turned to each other.

"Antagonis…" Narcissus began.

"Don't say goodbye, buddy, I'll be seeing you again, don'cha worry. We're bound to run into each other again in Hades," Antagonis said.

"I'm sorry again, Antagonis. You've been a good friend to me, and thank you."

"You're welcome, buddy, and no worries, it's all water under the bridge."

The men embraced warmly, and Antagonis headed off to the front gate, as Narcissus went off to look for Ameinias.

17

As he walked on through the fields surrounding the castle, Narcissus searched for Ameinias, stopping people here and there to ask if they had seen him. Narcissus found himself smiling at everyone he came across; they all looked so beautiful to him.

"Excuse me," Narcissus said, as he stopped one woman who was sitting on her own. "Do you know Ameinias? I'm looking for him."

The woman looked up at Narcissus, surprised to see such a handsome man with a wide, warm smile speaking to her. Her expression changed immediately from melancholy to bright.

"No, I'm sorry," she replied, standing up. "I could help you look for him."

"That's OK. Thank you, I'm sure I'll find him," Narcissus said, touching the woman lightly on the arm. He gave her another warm smile and then walked on.

As he neared the corner of the castle, Narcissus spotted Ameinias looking down at the ground, walking along, and dejectedly kicking any stones in his path.

"Ameinias!" Narcissus exclaimed, rushing toward him.

Ameinias turned toward the sound of Narcissus' voice, unable to believe not only that Narcissus was here in Hades, but also that he seemed excited to see him.

"Narcissus?" Ameinias responded.

"Yes, it's me. How are you doing? Are you all right? I'm so very sorry for everything."

Ameinias wasn't sure what to think. Though this man looked like Narcissus, he certainly did not act like the man he had loved.

"You seem…different," Ameinias said.

"I am different. It's all thanks to you!" Narcissus replied.

"What do you mean?"

"You asked the gods to curse me and they did!"

"Oh, I'm sorry, Narcissus…"

"No, don't be sorry. I deserved it! I was horrible to you. I just couldn't see you clearly, or myself, for that matter. Anyway, your curse was answered by Nemesis and I was doomed to fall desperately in love with my own image. And that's how I died. I just pined away until my body couldn't take anymore."

Ameinias was saddened to hear about Narcissus' fate, but he was happy that he had come looking for him. He thought that Narcissus looked even more handsome than he'd ever seen him.

"You've really changed," Ameinias told him.

"I was given the chance to see all the different parts of me, and I realized something really important: that there even *were* different sides to me! And, that I was treating people horribly just because of the parts I couldn't see!"

Ameinias had no idea what Narcissus was talking about, but

he was definitely pleased at this new version of him.

"Does this mean we can be together now?" Ameinias asked hopefully.

"Dearest Ameinias, you are a very sweet and loving man, and I am forever grateful to you for your love of me, and for your cursing of me. I do love you, but not in the way you love me. I treasure you, though, and I know that you will find another who deserves you far more than I do. Someone who sees the beauty in you right from the start!" Narcissus looked at Ameinias warmly, and gave him a loving embrace. "Are you OK with that, Ameinias?" he asked, searching Ameinias' eyes for his acceptance and understanding of their new friendship.

"Yes, Narcissus, thank you for your sweet words. I understand completely." Narcissus lingered longer, making sure that he hadn't hurt Ameinias again.

"The last thing I want to do is cause you any more pain."

"You haven't, Narcissus," Ameinias smiled. "Thank you for showing me such care. We don't always get to be with those we want, but I appreciate your kindness and honoring of my heart. It means a lot to me! In some way, it's brought me some closure. I feel like I can look again for love, even here in Hades."

"I really hope so, Ameinias. You're a good man and you deserve much love."

Narcissus told him that he had another stop to make, and invited Ameinias to join him, but he declined the offer.

"It's time for me to find my true love, Narcissus. It feels like the scar in my heart is mending," he replied, holding his hand over his heart.

"If it's allowed, please come and visit me in Elysium," Narcissus told Ameinias. They embraced again, and Narcissus walked off in search of Echo.

18

As Antagonis reached the gate, he was unsure what he would say to Herbavoris. After all, he was now free from that horror and Herbie was still stuck there. He reminded himself that he came bearing an offer of redemption, and it was up to Herbie himself whether he was up to the challenge.

"Hiya, Herbie," Antagonis greeted his old neighbor on the gate.

"Antagonis!" Herbie cried. "Where have you been! It's been so awful here without you. I've asked everyone who comes by here, 'Where's Antagonis? Do you know where Antagonis is?' and on and on. No one could tell me. So tell me, where have you…"

"Herbie, take a breather, and let me tell you."

"OK," Herbie replied.

"I've been on an amazing adventure with Narcissus…"

"Oh, *Narcissus*…what does *he* have that I don't? Wait, scratch that…he's gorgeous and he's not stuck on this door… OK, continue," Herbie said.

Antagonis took a deep breath and continued, "Listen, Herbavoris, I realized a buncha things on this adventure, and the biggest thing was that I don't always need to make people feel worse about themselves or their situation. So I asked Queen Persephone if she would give you a chance to redeem yourself too."

"You asked Queen Persephone about *me*?" Herbie asked incredulously.

"Yeah," Antagonis replied. "And she said yes, but..."

"She said, '*Yes*?'"

"Yup," Antagonis said patiently. "Here's what she's offering you: she wants to put you in charge of her garden. You must care for it and tend to it. But you *can't* pick the flowers unless she asks you to, and you *can't* smoke any of them. Those are the conditions."

"Oh, but they give such an incredible high..."

"Herbie! This is your chance to be free of the door! Isn't that more important?"

Herbie was silent for a moment, and then replied, "I could try."

"What do you mean, try? Why would you even take a moment to think about it?"

"I dunno. I've kinda gotten used to the door. Besides, I'd probably not be able to resist those lovely petals, and she'd probably send me back here anyway, or worse, down to Tartarus!"

Antagonis looked at Herbie with a mixture of disbelief and compassion. Herbie couldn't help who he was, and if he wasn't ready to face his own shadow projections, then there was not much Antagonis could do for him.

"If you ever change your mind, Herbie, tell one of the newbies as they walk past you to find me and let me know, OK?"

"OK, Antagonis. Thanks anyway for trying to help me. You're a good egg after all, ya know? You should probably go now, I can feel a scream coming on."

"OK, Herbie, take care," Antagonis said, as he walked back inside Hades. He listened as Herbie and the others on the door let out their blood-curdling screams. *I guess he thinks the pain he knows is better than the unknown, hmph?* Antagonis thought to himself.

19

Narcissus approached the Gates of Elysium and marveled at their golden glow. *How beautiful*, he thought, as he nodded to the gatekeeper.

"Greetings, Narcissus," the gatekeeper said, "We've been expecting you."

"Thank you," Narcissus replied. "And by any chance, do you know where I can find Echo?"

"She usually spends time over by the waterfall in the northern section," the gatekeeper offered. "Follow this path and you'll end up there. You can't miss it."

Narcissus thanked him and walked onward toward the waterfall. As he wandered through Elysium, the sites and sounds around him entranced him. He heard birds chirping and wondered to himself, *How there could be birds in Hades?* As he walked, he smiled to all those he encountered, and they, in turn, responded with a warm look and smile.

At the end of the dirt path, Narcissus came across a most beautiful sight. It was a young raven-haired maiden, playing with a kitten in a tall grassy field. The young maiden's hair glistened in the light, and her sun-kissed skin glowed as it peeked out from her light blue tunic. Narcissus ambled closer, drawn to the soft loving aura the woman exuded.

As he reached the edge of the field, the young woman turned her head toward him, and with a wide, warm smile, welcomed him to Elysium.

"Well, hello again," the woman greeted him. "You were on line behind me as we waited for the three judges, right? My name's Compassia."

"I'm Narcissus," he responded, completely entranced by her beauty and sweet nature.

"It's so nice to see you again," Compassia said. "Have you been exploring the Elysian Fields? There are some beautiful places to see."

"It's very nice to see you as well," replied Narcissus. He hadn't actually remembered Compassia from the line, because at that time, he had rarely paid much attention to others around him; but he certainly felt drawn to her now. "I just arrived," he continued, "So I haven't yet done much exploring. I need to find an old acquaintance first; her name's Echo. I've been told that she spends her time by the waterfall, do you know where that might be?"

"In fact, I do. I'd be happy to show you where it is," she offered. "That is, if you'd like me to."

"I would," Narcissus said gratefully. He couldn't think of anything more welcome than a walk with this lovely woman.

As they walked and talked, Narcissus could soon hear the sound of rushing water and knew that the waterfall must be close by.

After a bend in the path, he saw the magnificent falls. It fell in tiers, broken up by rock ledges, all convening at the bottom in a beautiful pristine pool. Dazzled by the rainbows dancing in the water, Narcissus gazed in wonder at the splendor of the sight.

"That must be your acquaintance," Compassia said, gesturing to the pool beneath the falls. "I'll leave you to your visit. It was so lovely to see you, Narcissus. I hope, perhaps, that I'll see you again."

"Yes, I'd…" Narcissus began, but he was interrupted by a sweet voice calling out to him.

"Narcissus?"

Narcissus turned and glanced toward the falls. There, bathing in the crystal clear water, was Echo. Narcissus smiled broadly at her and made his way down through the rushes to the water's edge.

"Hello, Echo. How are you? You look lovely," Narcissus greeted her.

"Thank you," she replied.

"And you're no longer repeating the last words I say. Has your curse been lifted as well?" Narcissus asked.

"Yes, Queen Persephone is not a big fan of Hera, so when I arrived down here, she decided that I had suffered enough and removed my affliction," Echo replied.

"That's wonderful!" Narcissus exclaimed. "I'm so relieved to hear that." Echo looked at Narcissus curiously.

"Why would you care about me, Narcissus? You called me a wretched creature and told me to leave you alone. Why the change of heart now?"

"I'm so sorry about how I behaved toward you, Echo. I realize now how that must have felt. Can you forgive me? You didn't deserve that treatment."

Echo rose out of the water, her skin glistening in the glow of Elysium. *She is beautiful, how come I never saw that before?* Narcissus wondered. Echo reached for a cloth to dry her hair and body, and looked Narcissus directly in the eyes. She wondered how he could have changed so drastically in such a relatively short period of time, but she could see the sincerity in his eyes.

"I do forgive you, Narcissus. Rest easy now, and enjoy your afterlife." She reached a hand out to touch him gently on the cheek. "And in fact, I've already found someone here in Elysium who has shown me only love and tender affection," Echo replied gently, as she gestured to a young man smiling at her. "Now that you are open to love, I know that you'll find someone here as well."

"Yes, I hope so," Narcissus said, smiling. Suddenly, a feeling of recognition washed over him, and he looked back up to the path from which he had come. "It does seem much more of a possibility now." Bidding Echo goodbye, Narcissus climbed back through the rushes and headed buoyantly toward the fields.

Epilogue

As Liriope waited in line to meet the three judges and find out her fate, she hoped that she might see her son again.

"Name?" asked the attendant, as Liriope arrived at the front of the line.

"Liriope," she replied.

"Please enter the courtroom on the right."

She entered the room, and greeted the three kings.

"Liriope," King Aeacus addressed her, "You've lived a good life. You found yourself pregnant after an unfortunate encounter, and yet you raised your child alone the best that you could."

"Yes, King Aeacus. And my son is here, somewhere in Hades. Would it be possible for me to see him, to know if he's all right?"

"He's just fine, Liriope, that I promise you," King Aeacus replied. Liriope heaved a huge sigh of relief. She was so grateful that Narcissus wasn't sitting in torment somewhere. "King Minos," King Aeacus continued, turning toward the ultimate judge. "I would like to send Liriope to Elysium, so she can reunite with her son."

Elysium? thought Liriope, *I was just glad he wasn't in Tartarus, but the Elysian Fields, how unbelievably wonderful!*

King Minos looked down at Liriope's happy face. "Yes, send Liriope to find her son. It'll be good for both of them to see each other again."

As Liriope entered Elysium, she marveled at the glowing beauty of it all. Walking down one of the many paths in front of her, she came across a magnificent waterfall. There, in the pool at the bottom of the falls, was her Narcissus.

"Mother!" Narcissus cried, leaving the water and walking hurriedly toward her. "You're here! I've missed you so much." He embraced his mother warmly.

"Narcissus, my dear sweet boy, I'm so happy to see you again. And … you look so different … so joyful!" she exclaimed in amazement.

"Yes, I am joyful," he replied. "And I want to you meet someone. But before I do, I want to tell you something. I know that I never said this to you, but I love you, mother. I love you so very much. You have always been there for me, and I've treated you like nothing more than a servant. Please, please forgive me, mother."

Liriope looked at her son lovingly, her heart bursting with love as she listened to her beautiful boy's words.

"Of course, my sweetheart, and I love you. You're part of me."

Narcissus hugged his mother again.

"And I have someone special to introduce you to, mother. I've fallen in love with the most wonderful person. Come with me," and he led her by the hand down to the water. It made Liriope so delighted to see Narcissus this cheerful and fulfilled, and as she glanced toward the pool, she smiled with joy to see the vibrant young woman heading towards them.

"Mother," Narcissus began with excitement. "I'd like to introduce you to Compassia.

And to this day, Narcissus can still be found bathing in the waters of Elysium, joyfully spending his afterlife with his mirror, Compassia.

About the Author

 Nicole Kavner Miller is an experienced lecturer, teacher, freelance editor, writer, life coach, and mythologist. She inspires her audiences and students to look beyond the ordinary appearance of their lives, and reach instead for the mythic - that spark of possibility and wonderment in all of us.

To contact Nicole Kavner Miller for workshops and speaking engagements, please go to www.nicolekavnermiller.com

39372278R20071

Made in the USA
Charleston, SC
05 March 2015